I0757485

# Slow Down and Let the Island Catch Up With You

Meet the Author and Illustrator: Amy Aanenson is a retired speech-language pathologist and a lifelong educator with a passion for creative writing. After retiring from her previous career, she recently discovered her talent for art. Writing and illustrating children's books feels like a natural path for Amy, as she has always had a deep love for children. She is currently working on her *Heart Series* book collection, which features original life lessons and her watercolor paintings. *Slow Down and Let the Island Catch Up With You is the third book in the Heart Series.* Winston Ekstrand's book, *A Place For Me*, is the second in this series. Winston is Amy's 18-year-old neighbor and one of her favorite people in the world. He allows me to slow down and see the world through his eyes. The first book, *My Wish For You*, was written and illustrated by Amy.

Printed in the USA.

ISBN-- (Paperback)-- 979-8-9998430-4-3
ISBN-- (Hardcover)-- 979-8-9998430-5-0

*Slow Down and Let the Island Catch Up With You*-- Written and illustrated by Amy L. Aanenson.
Illustrations executed in watercolor on Arches paper.

Summary- *Slow Down and Let the Island Catch Up With You* is the third book in the *Heart Series* collection. This book, inspired by the author's love of Maui, reminds the reader that intentionally slowing down and increasing your awareness of the wonder of the world around you is often just what the soul needs.

First printing edition 2025

Dedicated to my Maui Mama, Ruby Lea.
You saw the artist in me before I realized
that she was hiding beneath the surface.
Thank you for sharing your kindness
and wisdom with me. I will always
carry you in my heart.

Written by Amy L. Aanenson
Original Watercolors by Amy L. Aanenson

When the world is telling you to move faster,
that is the perfect time to slow down.

Maybe it is time to tip the hourglass on its side
and figure out some ways...

to slow down and let the island
catch up with you.

Slow down and stretch
into your morning.

while the rooster crows
with encouragement.

Go in search
of bananas.

Then lay out your beach
towel for breakfast.

Swing in a hammock

while you decide what
your day will look like.

Wander into the gardens

where you smell all of your
favorite tropical flowers.

Pick a bouquet to give to a friend...

and take some time to ask them
about their day. Listen.

Go into the rainforest and look
for the rainbow eucalyptus trees.

Soak in all of their rich colors.

Find a new trail to hike
through the bamboo forest.

listening to all of the
sounds of nature.

As the warm rain passes,

hide under your umbrella.

Time to go in search of rainbows....

and just breathe it all in!

Now take your kayak out and let the ocean carry you out into deeper waters.

Be aware of all that is around you.

Come back to shore...

and rest under the shadows of the palm trees.

Grab a beach picnic and your chair...

and end your day watching
the sunset over the ocean.

Now lie back and wait for the magic
of the stars and the moon
to appear above you.

Your breath feels fuller
and your body feels calmer.

Be thankful that you
slowed down enough
to enjoy the day and...

fully feel the love that
has settled into your heart.
Slow Down... Breathe...
Heart Series Illustrations
© 2025 Aanenson